From his home on the other side of the moon, Father Time summoned eight of his most trusted storytellers to bring a message of hope to all children. Their mission was to spread magical tales throughout the world: tales that remind us that we all belong to one family, one world; that our hearts speak the same language, no matter where we live or how different we look or sound; and that we each have the right to be loved, to be nurtured, and to reach for a dream.

This is one of their stories.
Listen with your heart and share the magic.

FOR SYLVIE AND
HER UNCLE RICK,
WHOSE CAPACITY
TO LOVE HAS
AWAKENED OUR
HEARTS.

Our thanks to artists Shanna Grotenhuis, Jane Portaluppi, and Mindi Sarko,
as well as Sharon Beckett, Yoshie Brady, Andrea Cascardi, Solveig Chandler, Jun Deguchi,
Akiko Eguchi, Liz Gordon, Tetsuo Ishida, William Levy, Michael Lynton, Masaru Nakamura,
Steve Ouimet, Tomoko Sato, Isamu Senda, Minoru Shibuya, Jan Smith, and Hideaki Suda.

THE RAGGED PEDDLER

Inspired by an Old Middle Eastern Tale

Flavia Weedn & Lisa Weedn Gilbert

Illustrated by Flavia Weedn

Hodder Children's Books • Australia

Not long ago, at the foot of a mountain, there was a small village in which the people complained and grumbled most all of the time.

They were never satisfied with anything they had
and were always arguing and unhappy. Everyone
who lived in the village worked for a living,
so they each had a home, enough food
to eat, and clothes to wear. But every one
of them thought that his or her
own problems were dreadful
and so much greater
than anyone else's
in the village.

They complained constantly when they
should have been happy and joyful
and thankful for such a good life.

They never noticed that in the spring and
summer the fields at the foot of the mountain
were beautifully green and that bright flowers
grew all around them.

And when the snow covered the mountain in the winter, it glistened dazzling white in the sunshine and glowed a faint rosy pink at sunset. The people never thought how lucky they were to live in a village that was surrounded by such beauty.

One day a stranger
came into town.
He was a peddler who
wore a ragged coat
and an old ragged hat.
He carried a tattered
umbrella, and a big
basket was slung
over one shoulder.

Around his belt,
a rope was wound
many times, and his
boots were patched
and worn.

He walked to the center of the town, then stopped and said, "Your mountain shines like burnished gold, and your rooftops and spires reflect the rosy color of the beautiful sky about you, yet you are unhappy. Come sit beside me, all of you, I have come to sell you happiness."

The people all laughed and called him a fool. "You not only look like a fool," they said, "you also sound like one. You bring with you nothing but a rope and an empty basket. How can that ever give us happiness?" And they laughed even louder as they continued to scorn this stranger.

But the peddler just smiled, said nothing, and handed the rope to one of the children. Although doubtful, the people were a bit curious, so they all gathered around to watch.

As the child pulled, the peddler spun 'round
and 'round like a top until the rope lay upon the
ground in a pile as high as the basket.

Then he threw one end
of the rope to the opposite
side of the street, where it
caught on a tree, and
he looped the other
end around a post near
where he stood.

"My store is now open," the peddler said, "and I am ready for business. So all of you who are unhappy, bring to me your miseries and your discontentments. Place them inside my basket here and I will trade them for happiness."

The peddler watched the villagers as they whispered and talked among themselves.

"He's even a bigger
fool than I thought,"
laughed one of them.

"It must be a trick,"
whispered another.

Then a voice cried
out, "Let's do it and
see what happens!"

"What can we lose
except our unhappiness?"
said another.

So in spite of their
disbelief, they put all
their complaints into
the stranger's basket.

Then the ragged peddler took the basket and lifted
it onto the rope, where it balanced itself. Suddenly it
began to roll from one end of the rope to the other.

As it tumbled along, it dropped everyone's troubles.

Soon every cause for complaint had fallen out of the basket and was hanging on the rope for everyone to see.

There was the fisherman's

worn-out sweater . . .

the baker's red hair . . .

the tailor's cane . . .

and the flower lady's

tattered shoes.

"Now, good people," the peddler said, "you need only to do one thing. Each of you must line up and take from the rope that which you believe to be the smallest trouble that you see here."

There was a great silence among the people as they each thought about what the ragged peddler had said.

The fisherman looked closely at all the complaints and said to the tailor, "I hated my sweater because it had holes in it, it's faded, and one of the buttons is missing. But now I'd rather have it than anything else. I can find new buttons and patch the holes, and faded just means my sweater is a different color."

Then the baker spoke up. "What would I do with a cane or a worn-out sweater? I've complained about my red hair because it made me look different from anyone else in the town. But I see now that it is the same color as my father's hair. It is a part of who I am, and I should be very proud of it!"

Laughing, the flower lady said to the tailor, "Wouldn't my shoes look funny on any of you? I never thought of it before, but I could polish my shoes and they would be like new. I want to keep them!"

The tailor, looking at his cane, said, "My cane is strong and helps me to walk. Why ever did I complain about it? Actually, I'm quite thankful for it!"

Soon it became clear that each considered their own complaint or trouble to be the smallest one hanging there on the rope.

Quickly they grabbed their own troubles back, and within a few seconds the line was empty.

"Has each of you taken the smallest trouble?" asked the peddler.

"Yes!" they cried.

"Then be happy!" he said, and taking his basket and rope, he slowly walked away.

From that moment on, the people of the village never had cause to complain or grumble again, for they had learned a valuable lesson from the wise stranger who had visited their town.

And now this tiny little village, resting so
beautifully at the foot of the mountain, became
a happy and joyful place to live.

A Hodder Children's Book

Published in Australia and New Zealand in 1995
by Hodder Headline Australia Pty Limited,
(A member of the Hodder Headline Group)
10-16 South Street, Rydalmere NSW 2116

Produced in cooperation with Dream Maker Studios AG.

National Library of Australia Cataloguing-in-Publication data

Weedn, Flavia.
The ragged peddler.

ISBN 0 7336 0024 7.

1. Tales—Middle East. 2. Jews—Folklore. I. Gilbert, Lisa Weedn.
II. Title. (Series: Weedn, Flavia. Dream maker stories).

398.20956

The artwork for each picture is digitally mastered using acrylic on canvas.

Printed in Singapore